TULSA CITY-COUNTY L

S0-AAG-533

A Note to Parents and Caregivers:

Read-it! Readers are for children who are just starting on the amazing road to reading. These beautiful books support both the acquisition of reading skills and the love of books.

 The PURPLE LEVEL presents basic topics and objects using high frequency words and simple language patterns.

 The RED LEVEL presents familiar topics using common words and repeating sentence patterns.

 The BLUE LEVEL presents new ideas using a larger vocabulary and varied sentence structure.

 The YELLOW LEVEL presents more challenging ideas, a broad vocabulary, and wide variety in sentence structure.

 The GREEN LEVEL presents more complex ideas, an extended vocabulary range, and expanded language structures.

 The ORANGE LEVEL presents a wide range of ideas and concepts using challenging vocabulary and complex language structures.

When sharing a book with your child, read in short stretches, pausing often to talk about the pictures. Have your child turn the pages and point to the pictures and familiar words. And be sure to reread favorite stories or parts of stories.

There is no right or wrong way to share books with children. Find time to read with your child, and pass on the legacy of literacy.

Adria F. Klein, Ph.D.
Professor Emeritus
California State University
San Bernardino, California

Editor: Christianne Jones
Designer: Amy Muehlenhardt
Page Production: Brandie Shoemaker
Creative Director: Keith Griffin
Editorial Director: Carol Jones
The illustrations in this book were created digitally.

Picture Window Books
5115 Excelsior Boulevard
Suite 232
Minneapolis, MN 55416
877-845-8392
www.picturewindowbooks.com

Copyright © 2007 by Picture Window Books
All rights reserved. No part of this book may be reproduced without written
permission from the publisher. The publisher takes no responsibility for the use of
any of the materials or methods described in this book, nor for the products thereof.

Printed in the United States of America.

Library of Congress Cataloging-in-Publication Data
Donahue, Jill L.
Last in line / by Jill L. Donahue ; illustrated by Stacey Previn.
p. cm. — (Read-it! readers)
Summary: No matter whether the teacher orders the class by name, favorite animal,
or height, Zelda Zena Zipperelli always seems to be the last person.
ISBN-13: 978-1-4048-2415-7 (hardcover)
ISBN-10: 1-4048-2415-4 (hardcover)
[1. Individuality—Fiction. 2. Schools—Fiction.] I. Previn, Stacey, ill. II. Title.
III. Series.

PZ7.D714728Las 2006
[E]—dc22   2006003415

Last in Line

by Jill L. Donahue
illustrated by Stacey Previn

Special thanks to our advisers for their expertise:

Adria F. Klein, Ph.D.
Professor Emeritus, California State University
San Bernardino, California

Susan Kesselring, M.A.
Literacy Educator
Rosemount–Apple Valley–Eagan (Minnesota) School District

PICTURE WINDOW BOOKS
Minneapolis, Minnesota

Zelda Zipperelli hated her name.

No matter what, she was always last in line.

In first grade, the students lined up
for lunch by their first names.

Zelda Zipperelli was last in line.

In second grade, the students lined
up for recess by their last names.
Zelda Zipperelli was last in line.

In third grade, the students lined up
to go home by their middle names.

10

Zelda's middle name was Zena. Zelda was last in line.

In gym class, the teacher asked the students to write down the name of an animal.

Then she told them to line up in alphabetical order according to the name of that animal.

Zelda had written down zebra.

14

Zelda was last in line.

On the last day of school, the teacher brought chocolate cupcakes. She had the students line up by height.

17

Zelda was the tallest one in her class.

As the students lined up to get a cupcake, Zelda was last in line.

Zelda patiently waited for her cupcake.
Finally, it was her turn.

Then Zelda's luck changed. The teacher had an extra cupcake. She gave it to Zelda for being patient.

Now Zelda Zipperelli doesn't mind being last in line. Sometimes, just sometimes, it's not so bad after all!

More *Read-it!* Readers

Bright pictures and fun stories help you practice your reading skills. Look for more books at your level.

Bears on Ice 1-4048-1577-5
The Bossy Rooster 1-4048-0051-4
The Camping Scare 1-4048-2405-7
Dust Bunnies 1-4048-1168-0
Emily's Pictures 1-4048-2409-X
Flying with Oliver 1-4048-1583-X
Frog Pajama Party 1-4048-1170-2
Galen's Camera 1-4048-1610-0
Jack's Party 1-4048-0060-3
The Lifeguard 1-4048-1584-8
Mike's Night-light 1-4048-1726-3
Nate the Dinosaur 1-4048-1728-X
One Up for Brad 1-4048-2418-9
The Playground Snake 1-4048-0556-7
Recycled! 1-4048-0068-9
Robin's New Glasses 1-4048-1587-2
The Sassy Monkey 1-4048-0058-1
The Treasure Map 1-4048-2416-2
Tuckerbean 1-4048-1591-0
What's Bugging Pamela? 1-4048-1189-3

Looking for a specific title or level? A complete list of *Read-it!* Readers is available on our Web site:
www.picturewindowbooks.com